Only just turned eighteen and now a growing author, Hayley had an incredibly challenging time growing up. She learnt independence and dedication within the strength of her own mind, enabling her to thrive at the start of her adult life. She lived a very different life in comparison to the people around her, and in some ways, this has formed both the good and bad with in her.

Hayley Sims

Dear Anonymous

Austin Macauley Publishers™
LONDON • CAMBRIDGE • NEW YORK • SHARJAH

Copyright © Hayley Sims (2021)

The right of Hayley Sims to be identified as author of this work has been asserted by the author in accordance with section 77 and 78 of the Copyright, Designs and Patents Act 1988.

All rights reserved. No part of this publication may be reproduced, stored in a retrieval system, or transmitted in any form or by any means, electronic, mechanical, photocopying, recording, or otherwise, without the prior permission of the publishers.

Any person who commits any unauthorised act in relation to this publication may be liable to criminal prosecution and civil claims for damages.

This is a work of fiction. Names, characters, businesses, places, events, locales, and incidents are either the products of the author's imagination or used in a fictitious manner. Any resemblance to actual persons, living or dead, or actual events is purely coincidental.

A CIP catalogue record for this title is available from the British Library.

ISBN 9781398409415 (Paperback)
ISBN 9781398409422 (ePub e-book)

www.austinmacauley.com

First Published (2021)
Austin Macauley Publishers Ltd
25 Canada Square
Canary Wharf
London
E14 5LQ

I would like to thank considerably the following: my dad for contributing payments in order for my book to be produced; Austin Macauley Publishers for taking the time and effort to help produce this book; my amazing sixth form English teachers, Miss Angel and Miss Marden, for believing in my writing skills! And lastly, to anyone who contributed to the events that my book consists of – a massive thank you for your bravery and trust in me for being able to put your experiences into words!

1. Numb to the Pain

She sits. Alone. Her headphones blasting, pushing away the outside world and compressing her inner thoughts. It is such a melancholy thing; for one to feel undead but living at the same time – for the robotic nature of our bodies to power through the days of exhaustion and uncanny, same routines, but to be physically, gently, breathing as her chest rises and falls with ease and grace, and her heart thumps with innocent life. Unquestionably, she does not want to die, but must she keep living? This is an overwhelming conundrum of forceful, uncontrollable and sinful thoughts; they feed on joyfulness, bravery and sincerity. Of course, she shines brighter than a shooting star, majestic and wishful, but her core is smoking, burning to the ground as her world practically shatters around her. Does she continue? Does she not? It is the over burdening question that flows like deadly electricity through her nerves and spins out of control in her brain. Various thoughts fill like molten lava to her brain's withstanding compacity, ensuring the ultimate eruption soon. Frantically, she pours the water of positive thoughts to steam it out – but what is it worth when fire meets fate?

2. In the Shadows

When she's happy, she's in golden glory; but when she's sad, she's a bottomless, dark pit of despair. There really is no in-between. Is this normal? Is this abnormal? The worries utterly consume her and shriek inside her mind, clawing to escape. It is the ultimate war between vicious demons and heroic angels on the drained mind.

Little by little, the depressive thoughts fill her up like a bottle of poison, sucking the pure life out of her. Her head is a storm, aggressive and dark; thunder shakes her mind as the lightning strikes, shocking her into a paralytic state; shackles of her forged prison rattle and scream; *Is this the end?*

Shuddering the house, screams of abuse are catapulted at her, as they scream and cry until their throat burns like the taste of vodka pouring down all at once. Families are supposed to love you, so why do they anything but? Is she this excessive burden? One by one, the insults are thrown, punched, kicked and slapped at her, as she stands there utterly broken on the inside.

Death is as a white lily, slow and painful; caught up in the battle of eternity and past, time stops at each passing comment, as she dwells and procrastinates. Must her life be lived within a time frame of toxic routines?

Her skin is a chilling cold winter, as the snowflakes fall from her eyes, down her bright pink cheeks as the numbness fills her veins; transporting it through her stiff body. Slithering into her bloodstream, you would have thought it would turn it a sinful black, potent and evil; hissing and snapping at all the pure features of her, as it replaced with a demonic presence. Her bones become hollow and cheek, protruding darkness and fear; with sunken eyes that demand happiness.

3. Heartbreaker

I silently scream, as the voice in the back of my head is crying for help, while the voice in the front is trying to supress these hurtful feelings. The more I do this, the more my chest squirms and tightens until my lungs refuse to breathe any longer. And when it reaches this drastic point, they gasp for air, clinging to the oxygen particles for their own dear life. Shaking and sickness rise from my adrenaline glands, as the anxiety floods in, as I remember the fact that I have lost you.

They say time heals everything, but this little broken heart cannot be glued back together, it will have large gashes of holes, unbearable scars and a tender spot for those who try to get close to it again. Because little do you know that the breaker of this dead heart has ruined the love and loyalty I carry, for the rest of my life. No amount of unbearable time will ever mend the gut-wrenching pain and sorrow I unfortunately now have. You say this is what is best, you say there is too much stress. But, did you ever come to think of my depressing consequences? You say this is all for me, but if it really was, why would you leave me so alone? I believe that no amount of sorrowful stress compares to the tragic heartache I feel. Heartbreakers are only good for their selfish and reckless reasons.

The memories come and go throughout the day, slowly snatching the left-over broken pieces of my shattered heart. How are you fine? Because I'm not fine at all. Montages of our dreams and memories continuously and vigorously crash into my brain, unfortunately reminding me of how you slipped away so easily and pain-free. The future that we had is now unclear and blurrier than ever. If I had one wish, it is not to get rid of our memories and experiences, but to wake up with amnesia to my sensitive emotions. To forget how it felt to love you, unconditionally, care for you wholeheartedly and without a doubt in my mind.

You brought so many colours to my boring life. You used to brighten the colour of the yellow sun, shining the light on my darkest insecurities and worries. Baby blue happiness on a summer's day, as we laughed the day away. October orange as we kept each other warm on our darkest nights. Pink passion as we expressed our love for one another. Ruthless red as we teared each other's throat out arguing. Gloomy grey as you betrayed and disappointed me. And finally, pitch black as you finally drifted away and gave up. It was the worst faded rainbow of my life. But the best brightest colours to begin with.

You express like a broken record, how you didn't give up on me because you'll always care and be there for me. But where are you then? Our relationship turned to dust and you're nowhere to be found. I believe you said this to make the guilt easier on you but more painful for me. You gave up, and now you must face that. The truth, unfortunately, is bittersweet and selfish. Stop pretending.

But, I'm better without you.

I will always want, care and love you more than myself combined. But I no longer need you, nor will I continue to foolishly chase you.

Because, I know, that if your heart was full of love and good intentions, our life together wouldn't have unravelled so quickly and unfairly. I thought what we had was real, but as you continued to shake our relationship, my thoughts of you lessened and shrunk. As I drowned myself, trying to swim to save you, while you faked on knowing how to swim, because you knew that I'd sacrifice myself for your wellbeing.

And I'm not saying that's alright, but I am saying I forgive you. I cannot hold onto this anger and hatred brewing inside of me, but what I can do is make myself the better person...

4. Violation

We laughed and joked as if it were the snippets of an old movie being replayed; appreciating one another's sincerity; in utter admiration of each other's strength as one!

Our connection broke, it faded and evolved us into strangers. But then you were back, as if the time that had passed had never existed in the first place. You were different, a shadow cast upon the past that was reflected by this emotion of hope that I had. The friendly face that I once knew had vanished and was replaced by this mask of evil. Our first night together, since not seeing you for what seemed like eternity, was ruined, violated and disgusting.

Your serpentine lips whisper sweet nothings into my ears to sooth me, as you forced your tongue into my fearful mouth. Slowly slithering down my body, you stopped between my legs and violated me – in horrific ways I cannot describe. My body felt paralytic and stone cold, but all I could do was scream from the inside and hold my breath on the outside, praying that it would all be over soon. Was this my fault? Why didn't I stop him? Why did I let him do this?

All these questions spun in my head, vigorously, as I made my way home from a night that seemed so innocent it turned into something frighteningly dark and petrifying. All I could do was feel *violated.*

Were you satisfied with your behaviour? That you stole my soul and corrupted it with such sickening stains; left your imprint as a wolf leaves theirs, making their territory which is most certainly not theirs to claim.

I can still feel your slithering lips scour my face and body, burning like acid, burning like poison, burning like the demon in hell you are.

You violated me.

5. Mania

Her mind is like a deadly disease, villains acquainted with one another, controlling her fragmented bones. Who is in control? Not her.

Vicious adrenaline pulses in and out of her veins, releasing energetic endorphins, dropping head-first into a pool of pleasure and content. The demons were at bay, silent; as her laughter excels and triumphs.

Suddenly, she begins to slip away, screeching down an endless sinister hole. Her mood flips. She becomes darkness. An empty corpse that still breathes softly and has a functioning beating heart but is no longer there. Who is in control? Not her.

6. Abandoned Innocence

Four years old. I remember it sunlight clear; your man back storming out of the front door, the aggression in your voice high but the loyalty towards your own daughter was painfully low.

You saw me every weekend for a few years, but out of the will of law, not the will of yours. Until, one day, the tiny adult in a six-year-old body said no more. No more did I want to be around this man who failed at his title of 'father figure'. He broke my heart much earlier before any boyfriend could.

I have your last name. I have your blood. I have your DNA. But I am still classed as the mistaken outsider to you and your family. I am shunned away from the surname that is rightfully mine, shunned away from the family that should've been mine. You were my unholy disappointment, but I was clearly the least of your worries.

My mother was a diamond – and still is to this day – continuing to shine and glow above your dullness like a stone; hard and cold as ice. She is as precious as the moonlight, shimmering and bright; you seem to be the black hole that sucks the life out of obstacles that cross your deadly path.

No longer the man I call father, no longer the role model I needed – but the wakeup call I deserved to appreciate the braveness of my loving mother. You are the coward that showed me to be better. This is the only 'thank you' you'll receive.

This is my statement as 'goodbye' as you missed out on the best daughter you could possibly have.

7. Insanity Consumes You

In and out, long and short – you were there so long that I began to forget what your face looks like. The worst part is, I'm contemplating whether that's a positive or negative aspect to your mentality. Your screams are deafening, screeching and penetrate through the atmosphere, smacking me hard in the face – leaving scrutinising scars and pain.

She says to him that she wishes and prays to god that he was never born, slamming the insults forward into his weeping eyes. Vivid hallucinations would consume her, separating her mind from her body, reality or not, it would all become an instantaneous blur to her. Her soul was lost in oblivion, entrapped by the walls of the place that is supposed to help and nurture her back to health.

Tearing me to pieces, our relationship becomes distant as I mature and grow – you still haven't changed. I fear that you never will, is it wrong of me to give up hope? Is it wrong of me to just want this nightmare to end and provide clarity? You're supposed to be my safe space; security; role model – family. To this day, I still don't understand what happened to you. It was as if a cloud of darkness snatched you up, carrying you away from us; as you went limp and let it. Why are we not enough to make you come home? It's like you're the female spectacle of Dr Jekyll and Mr Hyde; not even you know which one will appear at any second, ripping away the shred of happiness within me, unintentionally. I'm torn between the past that I want to keep; and the future that I deserve.

He catches his mother each time she falls, he even is the pillar that keeps her standing; no matter how much she tries to chop it down. Unimaginable wounds cover him, have become a part of him, but he still loves her. She screams until her throat burns, like strong liquor, but he still loves her. She dents him like a stone to metal but he still loves her. The overwhelming scent of his mother blinds him, as he convinced himself that this time will be different; she wraps her arms 'round him lovingly – but within a split second, pushes him down, shattering his hope, his heart. During lonely, dark, mystic nights, he dreams of a 'normal' mother, a loving mother, a stable mother; until the pain just becomes natural. She's a destructive hurricane, whirling around him snatching his happiness and stability; no longer feeling safe and sound.

Time passes in a whirlwind, as if I'm stuck in time, but everything else is growing. Stuck in this constant, deadly loop of uncertainty with you, forever alert of your next change in behaviour, yet my expectation of you still seem to be the same; hopeful and high.

Distance is virtue – between mother and son.

8. Social Services Solution?

He was only just twelve, barely even a teenager yet, barely even allowed his childhood innocence. It was cruelly ripped away from him by mindless adults.

Accused of sexual afflictions by outsiders, made to feel guilty of such things he'd never do, all pointed at him in regard to his younger sisters – who he loved dearly.

It was made into such a fiasco for this little boy, all the false allegations being cultivated into his brain, all the negative comments of abuse thrown at him wrongly! For an innocent child, it sure enough seemed to be made out into a dark police investigation, through the prying eyes of social workers.

'You did it,' they said.

'Tell us!' they said.

All the aspects of words being shoved into this poor, young boy's mouth.

'I would never do that,' he said.

'I didn't do it,' he said.

Bullied and verbally bashed, he still stayed strong, he remarkably told the truth constantly, but they didn't believe him. There was no sub-standing evidence, no witnesses, even his sisters disagreed. It was just the nosey neighbour who persisted. The verbal abuse progressed unbelievably, slashing not only him, but the rest of his family too. He would then lash out at school, his friends, even his own family; due to the isolation being placed on him for the false sense of guilt.

When all this nightmare was over, the weight of pain stayed with him through the years, forcing him low, down to the ground like a pile of heavy rubble. He chokes with tears of anguish each time a memory floods back; every time the word 'social' is spoken he flinches with fright.

What are we doing to this generation of youths?

9. Sociopathic Traits…

His relationships ruined; his emotions stuck in a time warp as he ages to maturity. His persona is unknown, his emotions lacking but his mind whispering, weighing up the angel and devil perched on either of his shoulders.

Deliciously charming and handsome, he had a smile that could make you melt like butter and ooze like sweet syrup.

Ruffled hair strands wiping across his forehead, messy and edgy. Smile as pure and innocent as the sunlight, as his piercings shone with it.

But his insides were pure black.

Stone cold and rock solid, his emotions were dormant, yet deadly. Unable to feel the pain he inflicts on others and struggles to feel an ounce of love back.

He is dead, but lives. He also lives but is dead.

10. Overly Obsession

It itches and burns, intertwines in my skin like acid and poison. It controls my brain and limbs, forcing them to do this inhabitable thing. Workout, sleep, lock the doors, close the curtains; workout, sleep, lock the doors, close the curtains… Repeat. I twitch and stutter and jitter and tense my muscles – all in the course of a minute, just sixty seconds at a time, which feels like a year to me. I chew and grind my teeth in spite, tucking away these draping urges and compulsive thoughts. My toes clench in fists, cracking and clicking the joints until they are sore and stiff. When will it stop? Why won't it stop? Can it stop? My mind races and dart from question to question, answer to answer, but it never really is satisfactory. My world feels like a misty, fast-paced dream, the images blurring by in front of my accelerating eyes as I chomp and chew my nails. My speech and vocabulary splutter and stutter as I ramble at one hundred miles a second. Workout, sleep, lock the doors, close the curtains; workout, sleep, lock the doors, close the curtains… Repeat. I can hear the clocking of my lifeline counting down, counting down until I go to sleep; when this misery ends. When will my misery end?

11. Addiction to the Physical Soul

Intimacy shows one's truest desire, to feel utterly compelled by nature and fully wanted in a singular moment. In one second, your emotions can heighten to the sky, as their fingers trace along her body; slowly but confidently. Her voluptuous lips, plump and poise; a connection vibrating through the two souls, becoming as one. To be gazed at, in such a way, in such a moment, is the desire to be loved and touched all in a millisecond, as their bodies collide like ships into rocks; unstoppable, quickly and instant.

They were both ravenous.

She was the fire in his eyes, the passion in his soul, the heat between his fingertips; while he was her water, soothing her ruffled ends and taming her attitude. Both elements are deadly as singular components, but together work in harmony to neutralise and sustain their boundaries.

Skin-tight but free, consumed within each other's worlds they broke down their walls to ignite the electricity between them in wholesomeness.

12. Here, There, Everywhere

Dragged from one country to another, a continuous loop of settling, unsettling, packing and unpacking; her world was turned upside down as she must repeatedly restart her life. A new country, new people, new phrases, new accents and laws; her education instantly harder, as she fails each one of her classes to begin with. A conflicted household of horrors makes it more difficult to find the comfort within the four walls of every new house she finds herself shoved into, cramped and unheard – lost but never found.

What next? she thinks. *Where to now?* she repeats.

She drops in, then out of schools, following her mother's wishes and desires, but she says nothing; no contribution to the decision, or the contributions her mother asks for – who then bluntly disregards them.

No money, no car, no house, no job – a constant struggle for the basic needs of life... all because of one selfish man who holds the power.

Intimidating and powerful, he strives to be the traditional "breadwinner" male, dominating the women in his life – selfishly wanting everything to be his own, spotless way. He's hungry for control and the ultimate way he does so is through money, the root of his beginnings of anguish. He stands over the trembling family with his dark, soulless eyes, almost blackened with his unruliness; switching from normal to intoxicating.

He is the epitome of disgust.

The environment is unsettling, lonesome and cryptic; all the qualities a loving home shouldn't be. From the bare cupboards, to the cramped rooms and the squashed space, it all seems to prove too much for her. She is the glue to the family, the peacemaker, who rights all the wrongs and improves all the unimproved; how can such a young girl do this? Resilience. Courage. Bravery. She possesses such qualities about herself that amaze others, she attracts the bright, shining light of hope that is rare; the pot of gold at the end of a stunning rainbow; a four-leaf clover hidden within the obvious gush of green.

But now she's lost.

Taken away once more, back to her home country. Leaving behind the broken, shattered hearts of her beloved friends here.

Back on the plane that brought her she stares, placidly, out of the rear-side window – gazing at the puffy clouds. She wonders what her life would have been like if she stayed in America. If she stayed in England? Her fingers tense, as a tear arises to her chocolate brown eyes, melting in the beam of sunlight that waves over her sun-kissed face.

Here they go again.

13. Trouble in Paradise?

When my parents split, there was some sort of weight lifted off my shoulders as I breathed a heavy sigh of relief. Having time with them separately was extremely fulfilling and special, I felt as though they had more time for me, more attention to spare without a significant other. Life was so relaxingly simple. Half of the week with my mother, the other half with my father, the ultimate balance for my teenage life.

I was as happy as could be, knowing that there were no more arguments, heartbreak, conflict. It was like a dream come true! I had finally awoken from the nightmare that kept me awake most dark, lonely nights.

Then, within an instant, it all changed.

My mother began dating again, which of course I was ecstatic for her, but things began to progress very quickly with one man. Within the course of six terrible months, he moved in. Without any family discussion or debate. It was uncomfortable beyond belief. Not knowing this man, how he would act or even speak. I couldn't lounge around in my own house without feeling concealed within my bedroom walls, forever waiting for him to leave the kitchen before I entered. I felt insignificant and dismissed, how could I have been left out of such an important decision within this small household?

Confrontation began, as disagreements evolved from this over-opinionated, forceful man; trying to cultivate me into his own idealistic approaches. My mother took his side, always. She had changed. Her mannerisms adapted, the household overly strict, silence of opinions and most of all, the death of my actual mother. She was replaced by some sort of a controlling stranger. I miss my mother dearly. My *real* mother.

Then, within an instant, it changed again.

They were getting married, all within the blink and batter of an eyelid. I was the maid of honour. How could I do this while bottling up all these feelings, forever forced to pile one on top of another. I could feel an explosion arising, from the pit of my stomach, churning, and the fire in my veins burning. I kept it in. Regret washed over me like a tsunami, thundering past me and destroying everything in its path. I didn't want this, I wanted to get out of this! I kept it in. My mind was silently screaming, banging, crying to be listened to, to be accounted for and appreciated. Nothing. I was practically invisible.

He would stalk around the kitchen, as if it were his own; swat me out of my own living room for his own preferences; force his opinions onto me at the dinner table, when all I was viewed as was an acquired hush. I was practically invisible.

14. The Struggle to Get Up

Approaching people, confronting his feelings, participating in his life passion – all put on pause for the demons that scream 'NO'. They're selfish and brutish, controlling his mind like a puppet master with dolls – whispering and feeding him the self-doubt commentary. They fester and burn through his skull, as he fights against them in a vicious and constant tug of war for the quality of life.

Physically and mentally injured, he keeps going, enjoying the small moments of life that matter the most. Battered and bruised, he stands tall, wearing the scars of achievement with pride and distinctive honour – he is a young warrior, battling the fear of the unknown.

On the outside, he is abnormally quiet, yet on the inside, he is like a whirling factory – full of excitement and life! His heart thumps and flutters at the thought of experiencing what life has to offer, filling his body with adrenaline and power! But the demons fight back. They intoxicate all that is good and kind, all the sunshine is absorbed with darkness and misery. How can something so small have such a large impact?

15. Behind the Scenes

Toxicity consumes them both, mixed with the idea and hope of love returning. But how can it? Arguments, disloyalty, disrespect. Once those qualities are lost, surely you have nothing? They both squeeze and hold onto their history and reoccurring memories as a comfort blanket, wrapping them securely within the confines of one another, distancing from the outside world.

She pushes, he pulls.

In a constant fight for peace, they're like magnets, switching from opposing to attracting sides. Brainwashed by love and their past, they continue, not knowing the depths of misery they have flung one another into. Solitude becomes them, drifting in and out of the real world, as they create a new world – made of fantasy and expectations.

It all goes up in flames, heat plastering their souls; chasing silhouettes; burning their throats like strong vodka; flesh melting at their intense voices. Communication is key. But they talk to listen, not to understand. Screaming would feel like the end of time, evil and dark, consuming all that is good about them both. He was thunder, and she was lighting; together they were an unstoppable storm; destroying all that is good.

But they can't live without each other. Their hearts ache when they're not together, pulsing to pull them back together in harmony. Sunlight clear, they light up when they are near one another, thawing their frozen hearts into warm puddles of water.

She was sweet and succulent as a summer strawberry, glowed like the rays of sunshine, beamed like the gentle moonlight. Her smile was contagious and breath-taking like a whirlwind. Petite and tiny, but still brave and courageous as a lioness, taking pride and value within her steps. Her skin was silk, soft, warm; eyes a dark, consuming green – like snakeskin; blonde and strong, capturing her undying confidence – even at times of insecurity.

He was bright and chirpy, inquisitive for all that life has to offer. Adventuress and bold, a chivalrous boy in need of support and partnership. Eyes like seaweed, salty and potent but completely mesmerising; hair as black as thorns, delicate and slick; he has the charm of gold, a cheeky smile that could convince you to do practically anything and everything. His words were smooth and persuasive, he was the ultimate character.

Perfect individuals, criminals together.

16. Lonesomeness

It's always at the pit of my stomach, churning and weighing my body down, forcing me towards hell. My chest falls with it, dipping after each longing breath; as my body drops and droops in unison. Like the life has been drained out of them, my fingers stiffen and curl – as they spread out in horror. My legs feel frail and weak, numb to their own existence and merciful wake. The bottom of my head tilts, unable to hold the heavy weight of lonesomeness that crushes it, slamming it into whatever object is within its reach; doing anything to relieve the pressure, tiredness, worthlessness.

My mind is a blur, full of zigzag, black and white lines that silence my thoughts into submission, separating my brain from my body. They flash in sequences, coming and going – as and when they please. It's as if I've gone brain dead but my eyes are still thriving, my body still moving to the beat of instructions belted towards me from others, as I mechanically nod to the beat.

My body itches and crumbles all over, as I frantically try to cooperate. Is this my body's way of telling me that it's over? Or is it another way of suggesting the torture still to come?

Dark rainy nights turn into hot, sweltering days – e
passing by while the hole in my stomach grows and feeds
the loneliness of my heart, aching and wailing its inner
sorrow. It feeds and pesters, growing like an infection that
never stops, never heals and can never be treated. It is
resistant. Constant.

Shut out like a disease, pushed out like a rodent, spoken
over like I'm invisible. Am I really that bad? Why is it
everyone who does this? Can I not have the relationships I
deserve? The routine had evolved into loneliness itself,
robotically repetitive and draining.

***Day one**: Wake up, eat, learn, home, eat, sleep.*
***Day two:** Wake up, eat, learn, home, eat, sleep.*
***Day three:** Wake up, eat, learn, home, eat, sleep.*
***Day four:** Wake up, eat, learn, home, eat, sleep.*
***Day five:** Wake up, eat, learn, home, eat, sleep.*
***Day six:** Wake up, eat, sleep.*
***Day seven:** Wake up, eat, sleep.*
REPEAT.

Is this really my life?

17. Where It All Began

The first daunting memory I have is a faint one, one that I
didn't quite understand at my young, toddler age. My brother
died. It was a cot death. I wasn't quite sure what had
happened, or why, and it didn't quite hit me until I was a bit
older. That was when the post trauma hit… I had lost someone
who I could have potentially grown up with, supported and

bonded with. I lost the only chance at sisterhood that I had. And subsequently, I was left with the pain of it all – the heartache above all heartaches, the one where you crumble at the grief of a beloved and lost soul; where the world comes crashing down at the minute of realisation.

It got worse.

My dearest mother suffered from a rare, hereditary stroke, leaving her helpless and ruined. She had to regain all her simple abilities and her heart stopped twice during the process. She is by far the strongest woman I know, living and breathing with grace and appreciation of the universe in her fingertips. I couldn't have lost her too. An angel in disguise, blessed from the heavens and sent down to protect me from harm, she did it all, miraculously and lovingly.

Once I started school, and my mother was in a relieving recovery, it was hard. I was distant, uncomfortable and struggled to make friends. They were harsh and vile, bitter remarks would slap me across the face, leaving a burning, hot print in their place. No one stuck up for me, even once. It was a never-ending battle to get through five insufferable years that I detested. I was made to feel worthless and invisible, and when I was visible, it would be even worse… the abuse, the insults and gut-wrenching damage. I would go home in undeniable horror – my lungs collapsing beneath my chest, my eyes drowning themselves, my body falling apart – crumbling my bones to dust. Every breath I sucked in would be lives knives scraping down my throat, clenching my oesophagus into tightness. 'Good morning' was painful to say, it was the ultimate lie, the ultimate pain within facing the day. 'Good night' was easier, the pain would fade, the thoughts would stop and the bullying was non-existent.

My mother's condition was unfortunately hereditary. So, I got sent in for tests. Lots of them.

That's when they found *my* condition. My brain was abnormally too big for my skull, pushing and pushing pressure against my head like a balloon awaiting to burst. Rushed into surgery, they operated, removing a part of my flesh and bone to make more room. The surgery itself wasn't disastrous, it was the aftermath. Having to have had my hair cut ridiculously short and shaggy, stripping away what dignity and self confidence that I had left.

This is my life.

18. Loss of Time, Loss of Identity

Time flies by like you're in a time machine. First, I was born and precious; then I was eight and mischievous; thirteen and moody; sixteen and lazy; 18 and a party devil. Then my twenties flashed by me like a storm of lightning. I'm now in my thirties and struggling. I did prioritise those little moments of pleasure and glory, when I had it easy. I knew myself as plain as day but seemed to have immensely lost that now in the present day. I've suffered a loss of time so great, that it's stripped my identity and who I was. Now I am a blank canvas awaiting to be painted upon, gushed with paintbrushes and charcoal, ink and pencil, smudges and shades. I've always wanted to be someone's muse. But I guess that life's not for me.

The years that have past, feel wasted and mutilated from the hopes that I never carried with me as well as I thought I did. Everything that was familiar to me seemed to fade into the oblivion, taking my soul with it. I quite frankly don't know who I am or who to be; the expectations risen against me seem to trump all the positives surrounding me and my progressing age. It's like practically waiting for the hands of the clock to 'tick' away every second, every minute, every hour of everyday; slowly and painfully to the day I die. Nothing ever changes anymore, the spark of life has been ripped from under my feet, leaving me helplessly on the floor.

Time passes like the abyss, unknowingly and swiftly; leaving you confused and uncertain. It picks you up and throws you around like a child's rogue toy, shaking you vigorously and violently. One way, then another, up and then down. The proportion of life you have is stained, tossed and turned, unable to be put back together from its cracks and shards. You're left cut, bruised and battered from the past that's caught up on you so quickly, unable to stop or pause the future from happening so vividly. My present life has yet to have a purpose, yet to have an enjoyable moment and yet to have peace. The idea of my past haunts me yet fascinates me, giving me some calmness of attitude. Don't take your life for granted. Don't wish away your youth. Don't miss out on the opportunities that you pass down from fear. Don't allow anyone to tell you what you can and can't do. Don't make the same mistake as me. You'll live the rest of your life thinking of the 'ifs' and 'buts' of the choices you didn't make or wanted to make. That is not worth it. Life your life to the fullest and never regret the dark parts of your life that sometimes cloud the light, it's a part of who you are, and you must embrace that. Don't be me.

19. Where It All Went Wrong

The wind gushing through his hair, the speed becoming a part of his body, merging with the engine and its ultimate power. Revving and bursting with fuel, he accelerates with magic and enchantment; his one passion and desire that he called home, safety. Adrenaline would sweep through his veins as he rode, breathing in the fumes of speed; it allowed him to be free and escape from the reality of this broken world. The thrill would take over, nothing else mattered; the gushing need for freedom and peace was his desire.

Then within an instant, it was stripped away from him.

Everything went black when he collided with a vehicle, dark and into nothingness.

"Man pronounced dead at the scene."

"Motorcyclist left with life-threatening injuries."

"Induced coma."

A bleed on the brain, shattered aorta, cracked ribs, broken wrists, half a pelvis.

Life looked slim, almost no chance.

"Hold on, we can't imagine you gone! We need you; we want you here!"

But he pulled through like a warrior.

He pushed through it, climbing through the dark tunnel and finally beginning to see the shreds of light – hope. His passion never went away, only his fear grew for what would happen to him next. It was a battle between passion and life, something that can never truly be decided upon.

Bruised, wounded, shackled with regret and shame; he lay there day after day in hospital, flashing by like a meaningless time lapse. His armour was in a million pieces, dented and in shrapnel; his wrists bandaged, his face discoloured, and his crutches lay by the side of the bed, mocking him as a reminder of his pain and long recovery.

Home. That's all he wanted. To have the safety and comfort of his own bed and four walls, without the closing in feeling that he was withholding at this very moment... He hoped and prayed for someone to take way the gut-wrenching pain he had, eating away at his flesh and bones, consuming him like a black hole.

The road to recovery was heartbreaking, difficult and pushed the boundaries more than anything he has experienced.

But he will survive.

20. The Desire for More

She craved adventure. Danger. Adrenaline. She was addicted to the thought of ruling the world, her independence and freedom all in the palms of her hands. She wants to feel like shock of life and its secrets, the life only others can dream of. To survive the unsurvivable, in the middle of the action. Become as dangerous, and venomous as a cobra – taking out her prey one by one.

She wanted more than just a typical job, a boring house and an average life. She desired *more.*

She didn't want to be a housewife, a job holder who follows orders, a 'work until you die' life.

Because in the end, is it worth it?

Is life the price we pay for our freedom?

21. A Night of Horror

A lot of my memories are faded and distant, from choice of blocking them out, but what this event is predominantly about is as clear as glass in my mind.

Society has seemed to cultivate this theory that mental health only affects adults, and depressed, suicidal teenagers; no one ever seems to 'bat an eyelid' at the thought of children also suffering. And I suppose this is what I'm here to subvert and change.

I was never really a happy child, I was always lonesome, left with no one to play with. I would sit daintily on the dim yellow coloured 'friend bench' as my infant school called it; no one came up to me. Perhaps that was the start of this growing snowball effect. It was as if everything in my childhood life started to come tumbling down after my younger years, as I progressed into junior school – timid and seen as someone who kept herself to herself. I almost fluttered through my four, awful years there. All of them consisting of constant bullying, taunting and verbal abuse. Things were thrown at me, confronted as soon as I walked into the classroom, teachers not helping or believing me. My nights at home would consist of crying myself to sleep, and waking up screaming in the morning, refusing to get dressed, clasping onto the door as my mother was pulling me out to the car.

At ten, I became ill. It was a mix of emotional damage and my poor physical health that meant my immune system was weak and frail. I came home, vomiting aggressively and constantly, it became so much that I refused to eat, my phobia of sickness arose and that's when the anxiety that I suffer to this day with, settled in. That summer consisted of smaller and smaller meals by the day, the repetition of getting up, lying on the floor and watching the television and then going back to bed. I felt physically sick every living moment.

I ached with the desire for normality.

It wasn't until my mother ran me a bath and helped me in that we noticed how bony I was, how frail I had become and how protruding the hollowness of my skeleton became. She gasped and went silent, leaving me to my hot bath. I sat there, running my fingers across my delicate hips, feeling the hardness of bone through my flesh. I did not like this. I did not even notice my decline.

I began eating junk food, day after day, desperately trying to gain some sort of weight, only succeeding in little amounts. I grew up into my teenage years, thinking that constantly feeling sick was normal, having a panic attack and choking every time I threw up was normal, feeling so depressed was normal for a growing child.

Secondary school wasn't any better.

The more it proceeded, the more I was overlooked and irrelevant, as if I was on mute to everyone but myself. Never the favourite, never the chosen one.

At fifteen I was at my all-time low, too anxious to go into school, too depressed to even care. It was as if I was already dead.

I wanted to be dead. I wished I was dead.

I couldn't laugh, I couldn't cry, I couldn't *feel*. I was so tired of feeling exhausted with numbness, with the only feeling I felt was the deep, aching pain in my chest that was dragging me down.

One night of horror, the night that I nearly ended it all...

In the pitch black, huddled under the covers of my bed, my humanity slowly fading, slipping through my fingers. I had made up my mind, I was going to do it. I collapsed out of bed onto my floor, crawling to my balcony door, opening it and breathing in the cold, chilling air. I looked down as my heart was beating to the sound of my inner thoughts telling me to jump. I moved forward slightly, preparing myself.

My phone rang.

It stopped me. He stopped me, soothing me, guiding me away from my intended fate. I am forever grateful for his intervention.

Because of him, I got to live my life, got to help myself and make myself better. I am still not whole, still not fixed – and I don't think I ever will be – but I am better. And I will continue to get better.

This is my story, the event of my life that affected me horrifically. But I still managed, coped and lived through it when I thought all hope was lost. I hope you will use this as your inspiration to keep going, keep moving… keep *living*.

22. The Turnaround

My whole life has felt unwholly and dark, full of misery and loneliness. But I have suddenly begun to realise my worth. The unsettling doubts still linger, don't get me wrong, they fester and boil until black as coal in my soul. Yet, I've learnt to live in the skin I was created in, realise that I am full of golden stars, worth a thousand diamonds and more. Worthy and special, golden and true.

23. The Older I Get

I used to wonder why they never could be happy, I used to close my eyes and wish for another family; the arguments, the abuse, the hurt. I used to be mad, angry, vengeful and hurt. Now I'm almost unfazed by it, I'm desensitised by it, used to it. It shouldn't be that way, I should feel something, anything – but I can't anymore. They've both broken me. A child should never have to endure the things I did. At a time, things were dark and scary, full of the inevitable, things still are, but I've adapted.

24. The Cheat

She was my world, my sunshine and flowers; blooming beautifully, she was radiant. My forever, I thought; my world I thought again. I imagined it all, the future, the wedding, the kids, growing old together. She was a narcotic influence upon my life, feeding my addiction to her, my need for her in my life – I feared that without her I would be nothing, irrelevant and nothing. Without her, I couldn't love myself, I kept telling myself that I wouldn't be whole without her, that my heart would be ripped out of my chest forever – convincing myself that I could never find anyone else.

My world came crashing down when I found out her antics, her deception, her unfaithfulness. I wanted to leave, but I couldn't, and I stayed – she thought I would allow this to continue. It kept happening, repeating and circling aggressively, it felt like a flurry of fists knocking me down and I couldn't get up. I didn't understand, I still don't, but I thought I was enough for her – but clearly not.

I don't know why I did this to him, I love him, but he's not enough for me – but I don't want to let him go either. It's selfish, I know that, but my impulse is to keep him, but I crave the love from others, I crave to be loved by everyone. I'm addicted to the attention, the love, the excitement and adrenaline of doing the obviously wrong thing. I'm caught up in it all, spiralling down like a whirlpool out of complete and utter control, it won't stop – I can't stop. I want him, but I don't, I don't want anyone else to have him, but I want someone else.

I can't drown out the nightmares of her with him, it keeps me awake all night, a growing insomniac. Sleep would be my escape, but then only for it to develop into my second prison, somewhere I couldn't run or hide from any longer, I had to face my demons created by her. Engrossed by her, continued by her – but ended by me.

25. Where's It All Gone?

Somehow, I've reached this point in my life where everything seems unseeingly boring – my passions, adventures and dreams don't seem to satisfy me anymore, I feel like I've lost the hope I once carried with confidence. I can't seem to focus, get things done, I can't get through a whole song, I can't get through a simple TV episode – all I can do is stare blankly at the wall and wish I had something to do, but everything I could do, or want to do, is supremely unsatisfying. I'm not quite sure how I've declined to this point, nor how to get out of it – as it just seems to come and go in waves. I wonder, what is my purpose in this life without my motivation and drive? My fire is gone, distinguished as the ashes lay spread across the floor in cold particles, the heat has vanished, the colour faded.

I've faded.

The repetition of my life has bored me, I've lost my touch, the touch that made me who I was in a special kind of way, I felt like I could stand out within the crowd and glow!

Now, I'm as dim as a blurry mirror.

26. Diamond

You picked me up at a stage in my life where I didn't even know I needed you, you came in like a gush of wind that swept me off my feet instantly. When I first saw you, you waved at me with goofiness, something that made me chuckle, I knew you were funny instantly! Meeting you that first day was like I'd known you my whole life, just doing the most simplistic things, sitting in a car park and listening to music, exploring the park in the dead of night – just us two. I told you stuff that I'd never told anyone before, because you attentively listened and cared, with only knowing me a few hours… you did the same, and I just felt this strong need to be there for you and hold you tight. Our laughter radiated from each other, my fingers intertwining with yours, I pulled you closer – I stroked your chin delicately, and moved my face closer, colliding with you – the most passionate kiss I've ever experienced. Everything felt right, our laughter, our jokes, your touch – was everything to me. Whenever I'm with you, I'm grateful, my mood changes drastically – the effect you have on me will forever leave my soul stained with love.

Her eyes are so bright, they almost sparkle, and she looks at me deeply, something I've never seen before in my life, something I thought only happened in the movies. Her hair is messy and perfect, it falls across her forehead in strands, first blonde, now purple – each colour making her more beautiful than the last. She's self-conscious, I can't figure out why because in my eyes, she's utterly perfect… her smile attracts everyone like a strong ray of sunshine, as her laugh makes my heart grow fonder and warmer.

Our first planned outing together was irreplaceable. I took her to the fireworks, somewhere where I could watch her eyes light up, like the way they do when she speaks about something she loves. I stood there, towering over her small body, looking up with her and my arm tucked underneath her, it felt like we were the only ones there, it was surreal and special. The explosion of colours reminded me of you in every way, the red made me feel love towards you, the purple made me giggle at your hair colour! Every time I looked down at you, a new way to love you came rushing into my head, because with you I'm not afraid, I'm safe and wanted – which is all I could ever really ask for. I took you by the cheek, and kissed you without hesitation, with no second thoughts – the fireworks kept going behind us and I knew you were the one for me, undoubtedly. I saw you, right through you, my diamond.

27. Unwanted

When you feel so unwanted, so alone, that's when you're at your weakest – most vulnerable state imaginable. Sometimes it feels like you're being stupid, that it's only your brain fooling you – but other times, you can see straight through the truth. You're not the first choice, you're not the loved one, you're hated to be precise. Maybe I fucked it up and my eyes couldn't see that, magnifying all my flaws in my head as I bat myself up, time and time again. But, then again, if you did something, surely you could recognise it? And understand why people hate you for the person you are? Find out what qualities about yourself to change…

I would never wish this feeling upon anyone, not just because of the consequences, but the pureness that it's so difficult to put into words, so difficult to summarise all of the words that linger in your head to transfer them to physical words. It feels like a malfunction in my brain, everything seems to be spinning, but won't work the way it's supposed to, maybe I'm broken. Sometimes, I ponder whether it would be worth it to completely change, travel to the depths of the unknown to start again, maybe I'll be loved then. I want to be loved deeply, not widely, just enough to feel secure within myself. It's almost as if, so much has happened to be that I either feel so numb that I don't even react to the situation – or something so minuscule happens that the tears well up and I already think about suicide. It's one extreme or the other.

I've lost so many people, I can't decide whether it's a sign to give up, or a blessing in disguise.

I'm a sinking ship, going down slowly and weighing myself down, but that also means I can't be saved, only remains can be gathered. I can't ever be whole.

I do something wrong in everyone's eyes.

28. Watching Your Decline

Your moods were inconsistent and made us all tiptoe around your presence. You're like a ticking time bomb, waiting for the perfect moment to set yourself off – destroying us in your path... because if you're not happy, no one else can be, right?

29. Left to the Dust

Scattered around like fragile ashes, burning holes in the ground as each piece of me reaches rock bottom. I thought you were my forever, but little did I know, forever meant you'd leave. I ache for you, your tough, your compelling scent and smooth skin; the weight on my shoulders getting heavier each second that you're not mine anymore. I hate to beg, I know my worth, but you're different than the rest...

Your honey eyes intrigue me, infatuate me with their exquisite curls and rays of golden specs as the sunlight hits them, your smile gradual but beautifully radiant and glowing, your hair chestnut brown and perfect. You beam with glory and beauty when I glance at you! But, my most favourite time to admire you is when you used to look at me, with sincerity and compassion. I miss that.

You're like fire, that burns wholeheartedly inside of me, consuming me but brightening me at my dullest moments. But you leave me in ashes. Frail and gasping for you, screaming like the hollow sound of death as the pain of losing you is unbearable. A life without you is like a life without lungs, you burned them away with your departure, as I'm left struggling for air, struggling for breath.

I would never describe my life as perfect, however, with you in it, I saw the hope in everything – every pitch-black corner was never too dark for me with you.

You left a hole, unfillable and treacherous and unfixable.

30. Too Sad to Cry

That emptiness that you feel, shrouded in your chest, piled upon and covered, that's what this is. When you're past crying, but your body continues inside. Your breath feels shallow and weighed upon like a ton; so that when you do finally take a deep breath, it feels like a gasp, a struggle for the air that you know that you can physically breathe, but you mentally can't contain it. It's like a bottomless hole that you know that you can't fill, a void so deep that nothing can be done; and you're left miserably wondering if this is what life will feel like forever. To depend on the companionship of someone else, debating whether you're happy or whether you're keeping yourself busy in order to feel this mirage. Even sleeping becomes painful, as you reconcile that at some point, you'll have to wake up and do it all again, and you wonder, is it worth it? The only thing worse than breaking down is being unable to. One more day turns into one more week, one more month… a repetitive cycle of survival – alive but not really living.

You can feel it circulate in your body, and I know that sounds strange, 'how can you feel something going on in your brain, in your actual body?' Well, I don't know either, but it does. You ache, feel the pulse, the drooping of your limbs, the clenching of your fingers and toes. It radiates throughout you. Rattles you. All consuming. You wish so hard to be content within yourself and your own company, but the loneliness hovers, dark and melancholic. The sickness rises, controlling every ounce of you, the urge to scream seems appealing but no sound comes out – only a moving doll can be seen from the outside.

31. I Want to Tell You That I Love You, but I Can't

I lay next to you in the hazy dark, while the world is silent and peaceful – you're fast asleep and your breathing is soft and pure. I gaze at you full of complete love, my fingers tracing your skin lightly as I automatically smile at your indescribable beauty. I nudge your head against my chest as you doze, you're so beautiful. But you're not mine – not in the way I want you, my soul mate beyond belief. Your soft hands sprawled across my thighs feeding my body warmth, all I can think about is how your touch enlightens me, it does something to me that I could never see myself having with someone else, not sexually, but intimately you show me a world full of bursting colours. I couldn't help but gently kiss you, tracing it along your back and head, my eyes appreciating every fibre of you. I fell for you more than I already had at this moment, witnessing your vulnerability, the real you. You wrap your arms tighter around me as you sleep, your muscles gripping me safely as I bury myself into you; I'm already as close as I could physically get to you, but I want to be closer, I want to touch you closely with sincerity and love. I want you to know how much I love you, how much I'm in love with you – but I can't for your sake. When I look at you, it's like I see my whole life in front of me; when my world is falling apart, I look at you and see hope if I have you. I don't belong anywhere else other than next to you, I lay here with the feeling of your bare skin on mine, and this is the only thing I can imagine… you. Nothing else matters, but you. You appear like a dream to me, real but just out of my reach – I must touch you to make sure you're still there. I don't believe that I could recover if I lost you. You healed me in ways I thought I was permanently broken.

But, we're just friends for now. Friends who kiss, sleep next to one another and love each other – but we can't say it, we can't touch the love yet, for your sake. Can't you see the way we look at each other, the way that we don't want anyone else, the fire that consumes us when we're together? I found love where it wasn't supposed to be, right in front of me, not knowing how much you'd mean to me over the course of four months so far… what're you doing to me?

32. Would It Be Easier If I Just Left?

I crave to live, to experience the unknown but 'm stuck in my skin, such scratching at it, pining to escape from myself. I have desires, dreams and the idea of how I want to live my life – but I don't want to live it. It's almost as if I have these ideals set out for someone else, someone that is not me. I want to die. It is plain and simple. But I have the fear of missing out, I wonder whether things get easier, whether things change, or things adapt, and I'm just not sure anymore. Can I figure this out? I'm not sure I can anymore.